Peanut-Free Tea for Three

For hosts and favorite guests,
especially kids with peanut allergies,
who know how to party best!

LIBRARY OF CONGRESS CONTROL NUMBER: 2009903027
ISBN 978-0-9822150-1-2

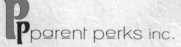

parent perks inc.

P.O. Box 95024
Newton, Massachusetts 02495
www.parentperksinc.com

Authors: Heather Mehra and Kerry McManama
Illustrations: ©Michael Kline Illustration (dogfoose.com)
Design: JoeLeeDesign.com
Printed in China

the **No Biggie bunch** ™

Peanut-Free Tea for Three

BY
Heather Mehra & Kerry McManama

ILLUSTRATIONS BY
Michael Kline

Legumenot

FOR KIDS CREATIVELY COPING WITH FOOD ALLERGIES

Paige and Greta arrived at Eliot's house for a dress-up tea party. "C'mon, let's put on our hats and get started!" Paige said.

"I've got my No Biggie Bag," Greta told Eliot and Paige. "Everything I need is inside. I'm coming from outer space so I brought my helmet," Greta said. Paige watched Greta put on her space helmet.

"Can you really drink tea
with that thing on?"

Greta answered in her astronaut voice. "The visor lifts up. See? Open, shut!"

Eliot showed the girls the surprises in his No Biggie Bag next. He unbuckled it and pulled out his cowboy hat, egg-free rice cakes and a jar of jelly. He flipped on his hat. "Are you ready for tea and snacks? Gluten-free, for Greta!" he said.

Astronaut Greta's helmet nodded. Eliot and Paige heard a muffled, "Yes!" from inside. "Me, too!" Princess Paige agreed as she adjusted her crown.

Eliot rounded up his tea party posse. He carefully poured juice into little tin teacups. "Cowboy juice," Eliot said as he tipped his hat. "Who wants a rice cake with jelly?"

"I do!" Greta said as she took off her helmet. "But we can't use your jelly, cowboy."

"There could be traces of peanuts in there from the last time somebody made a peanut butter and jelly sandwich. Remember, Paige is allergic to peanuts," Greta explained.

"No biggie!"

"Along with my princess crown,
I packed my own jelly in my
No Biggie Bag. It's strawberry!"

"Yum, strawberry jelly!" Eliot said. "You're always prepared, Paige. Just like me. I have to be. I'm allergic to eggs."

The No Biggie Bunch enjoyed the super-cool tea party with their safe and tasty snacks.

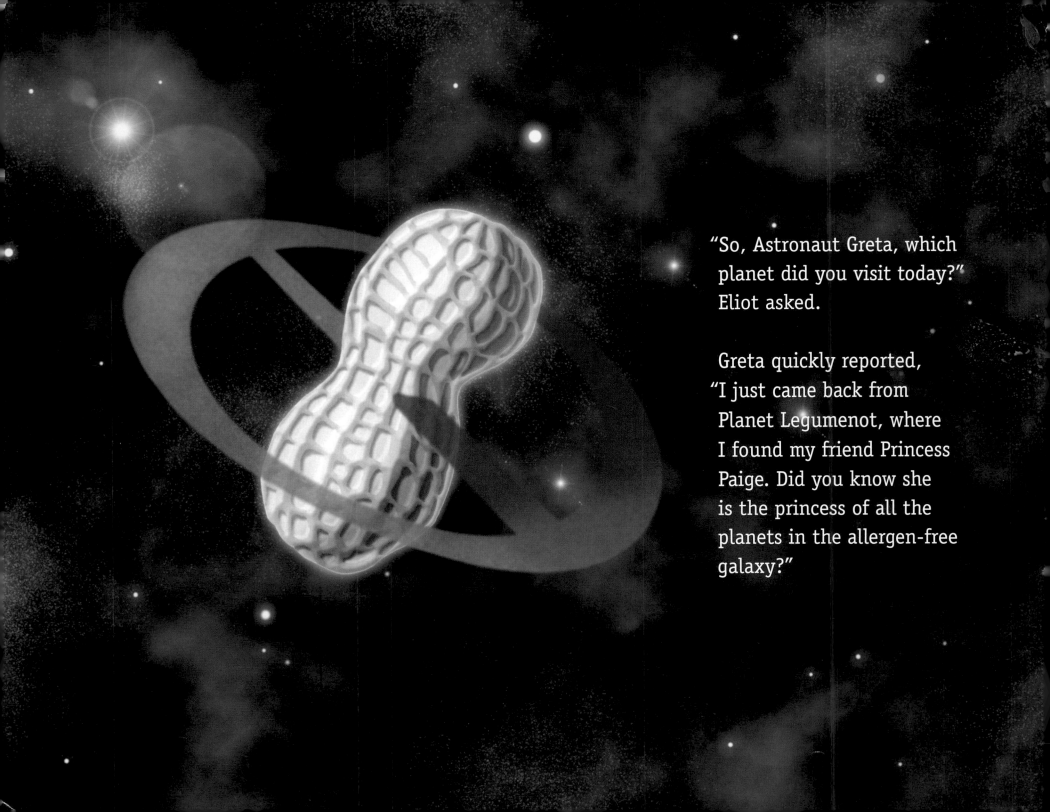

"So, Astronaut Greta, which
planet did you visit today?"
Eliot asked.

Greta quickly reported,
"I just came back from
Planet Legumenot, where
I found my friend Princess
Paige. Did you know she
is the princess of all the
planets in the allergen-free
galaxy?"

"Thanks for the cowboy juice and the jelly rice cakes," Princess Paige told Cowboy Eliot. "They taste better than anything we have on Planet Legumenot!"

"Yee-haw!"

The No Biggie Bunch tea-partied on.

No Biggie Bag Bonus

What would you pack in your
No Biggie Bag for a dress-up tea party?

Yummy
strawberry jelly

Super astronaut
helmet

Crunchy
rice cakes

Greta

Greetings from outer space! I'm Greta. I'm allergic to gluten.

Scotty

Hey, sports fans! My name is Scotty. I'm allergic to Soy.

Paige

I'm Paige, the fairest princess in all the land. I'm allergic to peanuts.

Meet the No Biggie Bunch

Davis

Hello, fellow explorers. I'm Davis and I love dinosaurs. I'm allergic to dairy.

Natalie

Hi, friends. My name is Natalie and I'm artsy. I have no food allergies.

Eliot

Howdy, partners! They call me Cowboy Eliot. I'm allergic to egg.

The Mission of the No Biggie Bunch

The No Biggie Bunch is a diverse group of kids who handle the social challenges of food allergies with poise and panache.

The adventures of Davis, Natalie, Paige, Eliot, Scotty and Greta are neither technical nor medical. Their stories are meant to act as springboards for conversation among children, parents, teachers, friends and family members.

The No Biggie Bunch doesn't speak about limitations or medications. They focus on allergen-free celebrations and smart preparation.

Focus on fun and all you can do and soon you'll be saying,

"No Biggie" too!